Dear Parent:

Congratulations! Your child is taking the first steps on an exciting journey. The destination? Independent reading!

STEP INTO READING® will help your child get there. The program offers five steps to reading success. Each step includes fun stories and colorful art. There are also Step into Reading Sticker Books, Step into Reading Math Readers, Step into Reading Phonics Readers, Step into Reading Write-In Readers, and Step into Reading Phonics Boxed Sets—a complete literacy program with something to interest every child.

Learning to Read, Step by Step!

Ready to Read Preschool–Kindergarten
• big type and easy words • rhyme and rhythm • picture clues
For children who know the alphabet and are eager to begin reading.

Reading with Help Preschool–Grade 1
• basic vocabulary • short sentences • simple stories
For children who recognize familiar words and sound out new words with help.

Reading on Your Own Grades 1–3
• engaging characters • easy-to-follow plots • popular topics
For children who are ready to read on their own.

Reading Paragraphs Grades 2–3
• challenging vocabulary • short paragraphs • exciting stories
For newly independent readers who read simple sentences with confidence.

Ready for Chapters Grades 2–4
• chapters • longer paragraphs • full-color art
For children who want to take the plunge into chapter books but still like colorful pictures.

STEP INTO READING® is designed to give every child a successful reading experience. The grade levels are only guides. Children can progress through the steps at their own speed, developing confidence in their reading, no matter what their grade.

Remember, a lifetime love of reading starts with a single step!

For Pugs
—D.R.S.

To my wife and daughter,
the super heroes in my life
—P.S.

Visit us on the Web!
www.stepintoreading.com
www.randomhouse.com/kids
www.marvel.com

Educators and librarians, for a variety of teaching tools, visit us at
www.randomhouse.com/teachers

Library of Congress Cataloging-in-Publication Data

Shealy, Dennis R.
Whiplash! / adapted by Dennis R. Shealy ; illustrated by Patrick Spaziante.
p. cm. — (Step into reading. Step 3)
"Based on the episode 'Whiplash' by Paul Giacoppo."
ISBN 978-0-375-86452-0 (trade) — ISBN 978-0-375-96452-7 (Gibraltar library binding)
I. Spaziante, Patrick. II. Iron Man (Television program). III. Title.
PZ7.S53767Wh 2010v
[E]—dc22
2009029555

Printed in the United States of America
10 9 8 7 6 5

IRON MAN™
ARMORED ADVENTURES
WHIPLASH!

Adapted by D. R. Shealy
Based on the episode "Whiplash,"
by Paul Giacoppo
Illustrated by Patrick Spaziante

Random House 🏠 New York

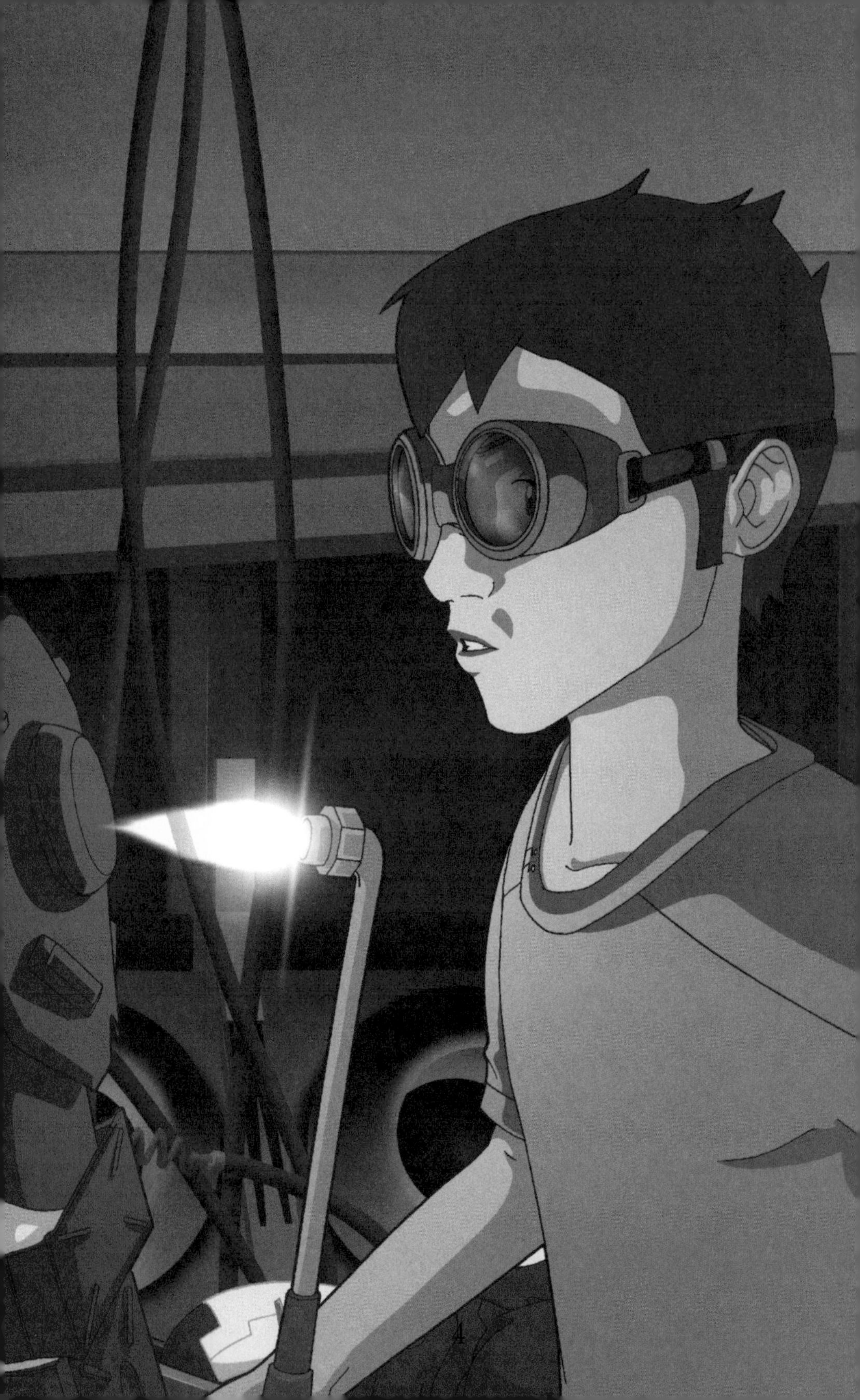

High school student

Tony Stark

has an amazing secret:

he is really the armored super hero

Iron Man!

Tony's best friend,
James "Rhodey" Rhodes,
knows his secret.
Rhodey helps Tony
fight the bad guys.

Today

Rhodey is helping Tony

get to school

on time!

Tony shows Rhodey

his new battle glove.

It will make

his armor more powerful.

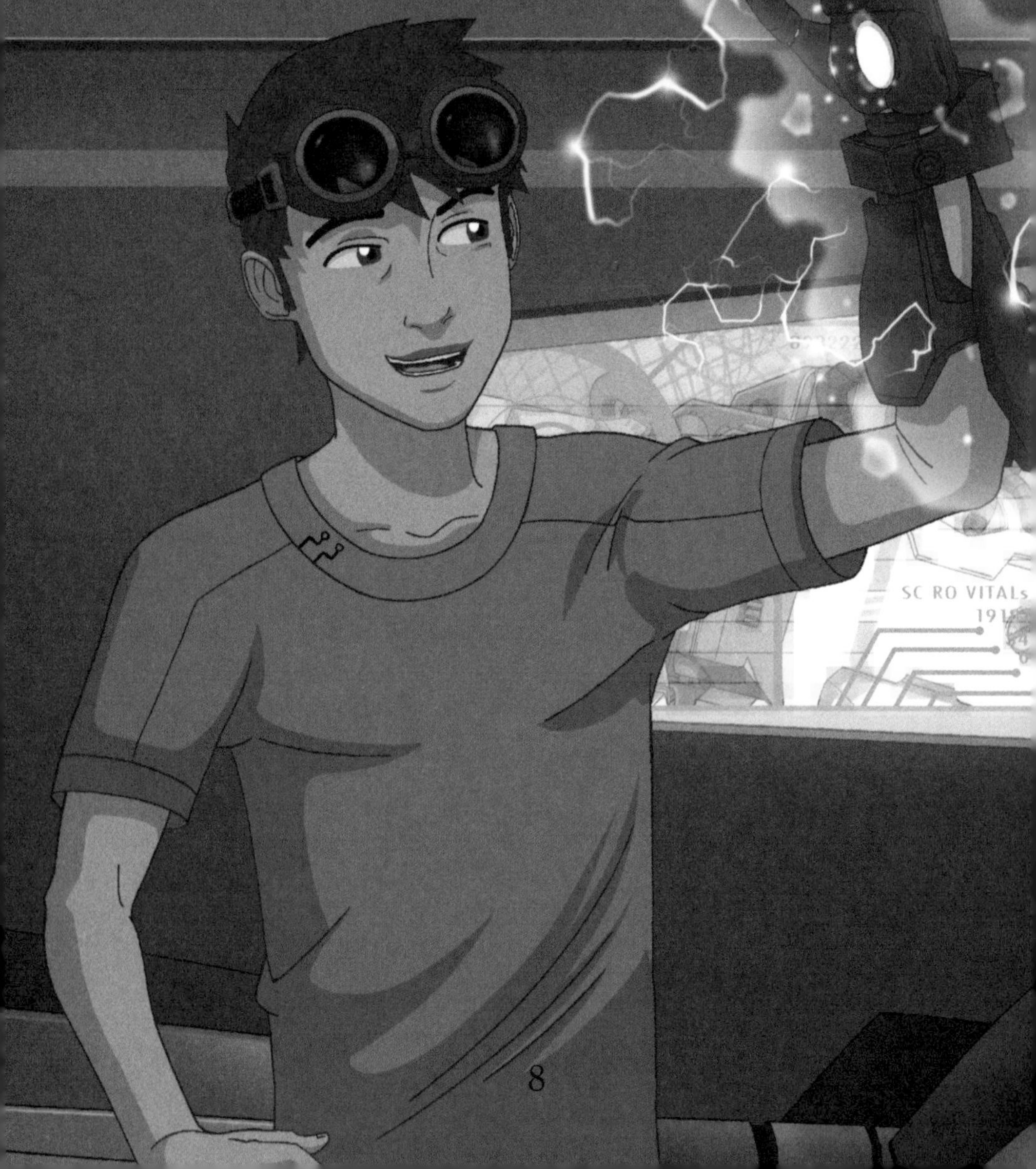

The bad guys' weapons

keep getting better.

Tony wants to know

who is making them.

Tony and Rhodey

go to class.

Secret agents lead

their friend Pepper Potts away.

"My father has been hurt,"

she says.

"He was looking for

someone named Mr. Fix!"

The agents take

Pepper home

to protect her.

Pepper searches

her father's computer.

She wants to learn more

about Mr. Fix.

But Mr. Fix is
using his computer
to spy on Pepper.

"Stop her!"

Mr. Fix tells his thugs.

Mr. Fix's thugs

knock down the door

of Pepper's house.

Pepper grabs her phone

and runs!

She calls

Rhodey for help.

Rhodey tells Tony
that Pepper is in trouble.
Iron Man
is on the way!

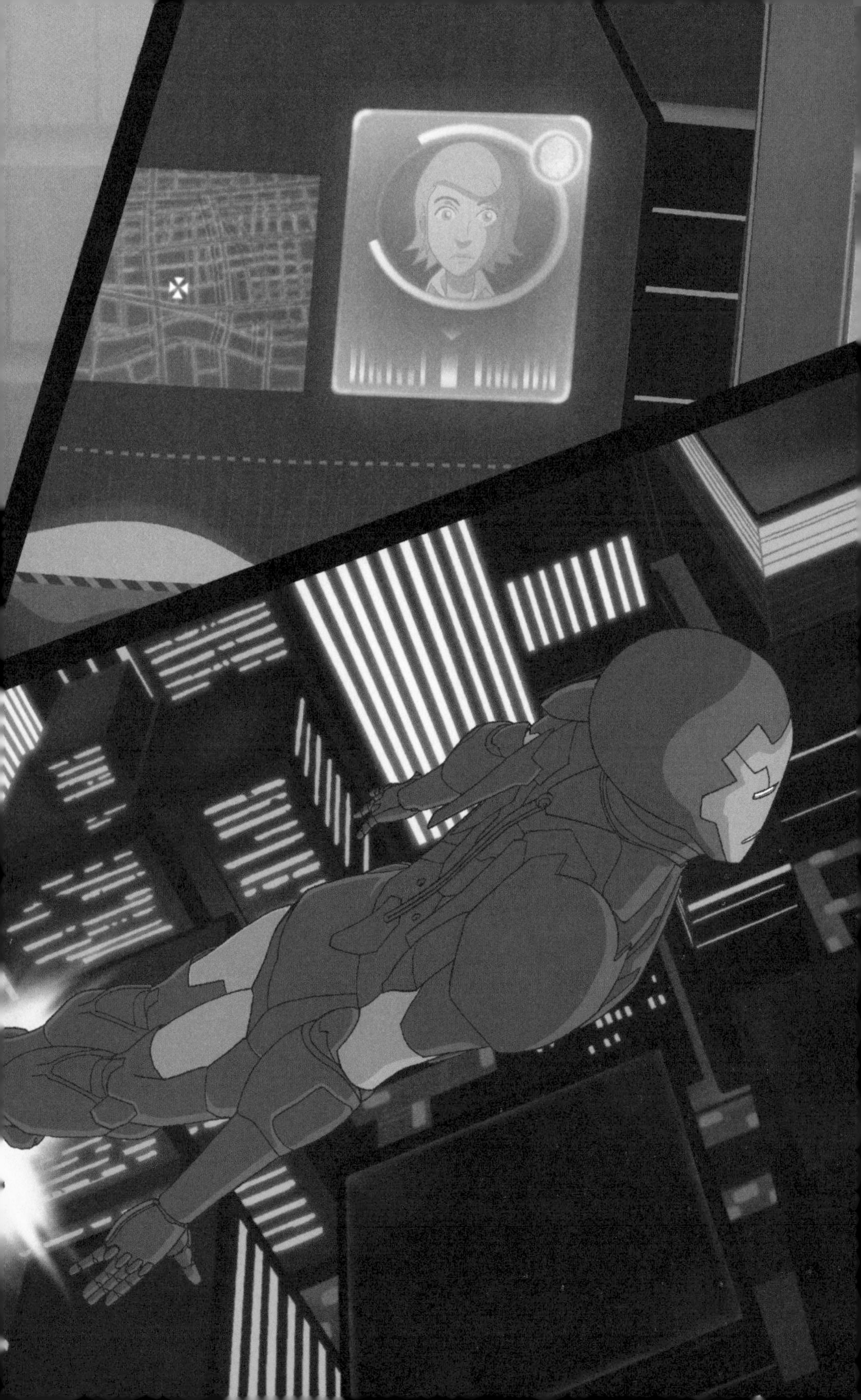

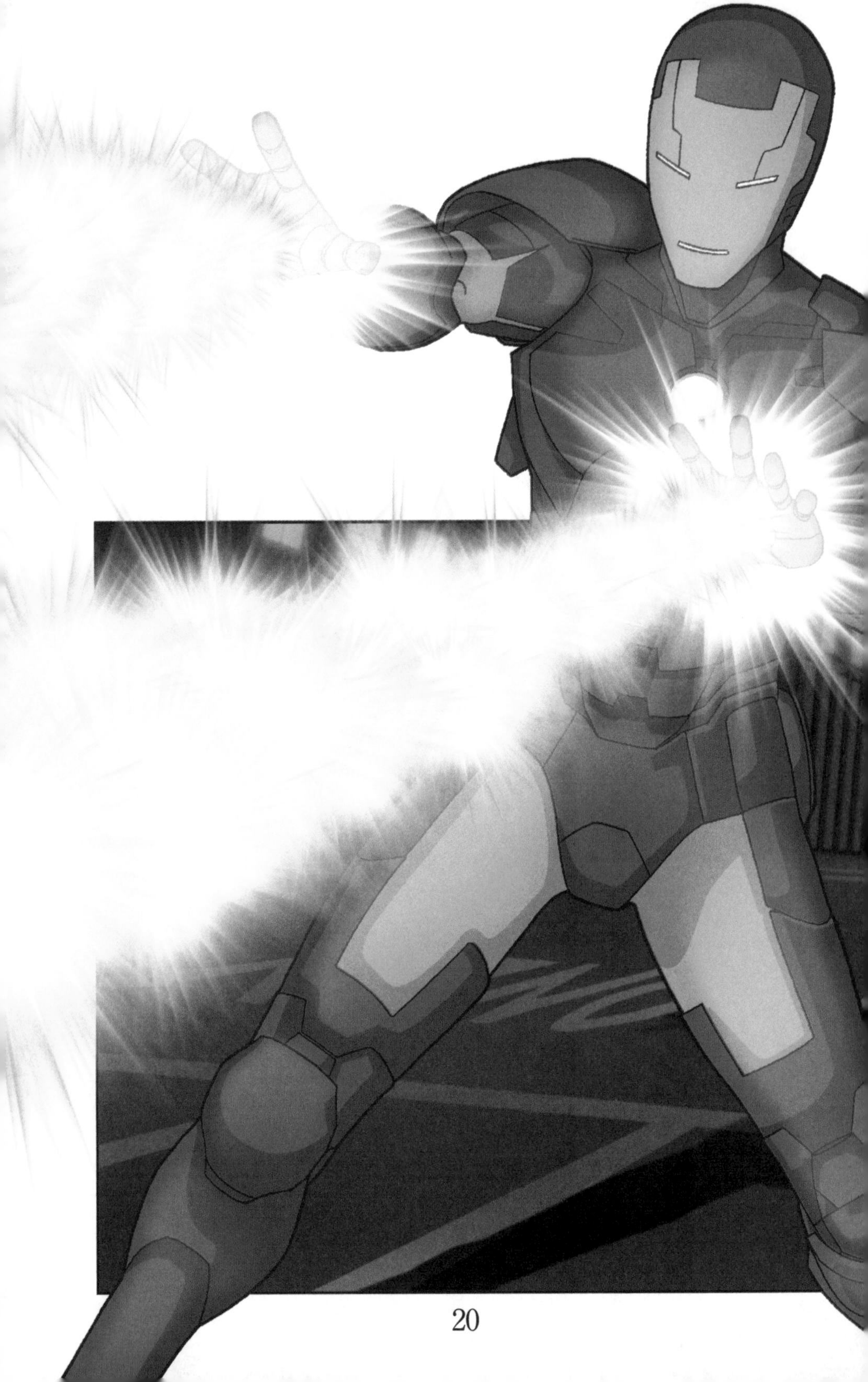

Iron Man lands

between the thugs

and Pepper.

He stuns the thugs

with his repulsor rays!

Iron Man grabs Pepper and
soars into the sky.
"Thanks, Tony!"
she says.

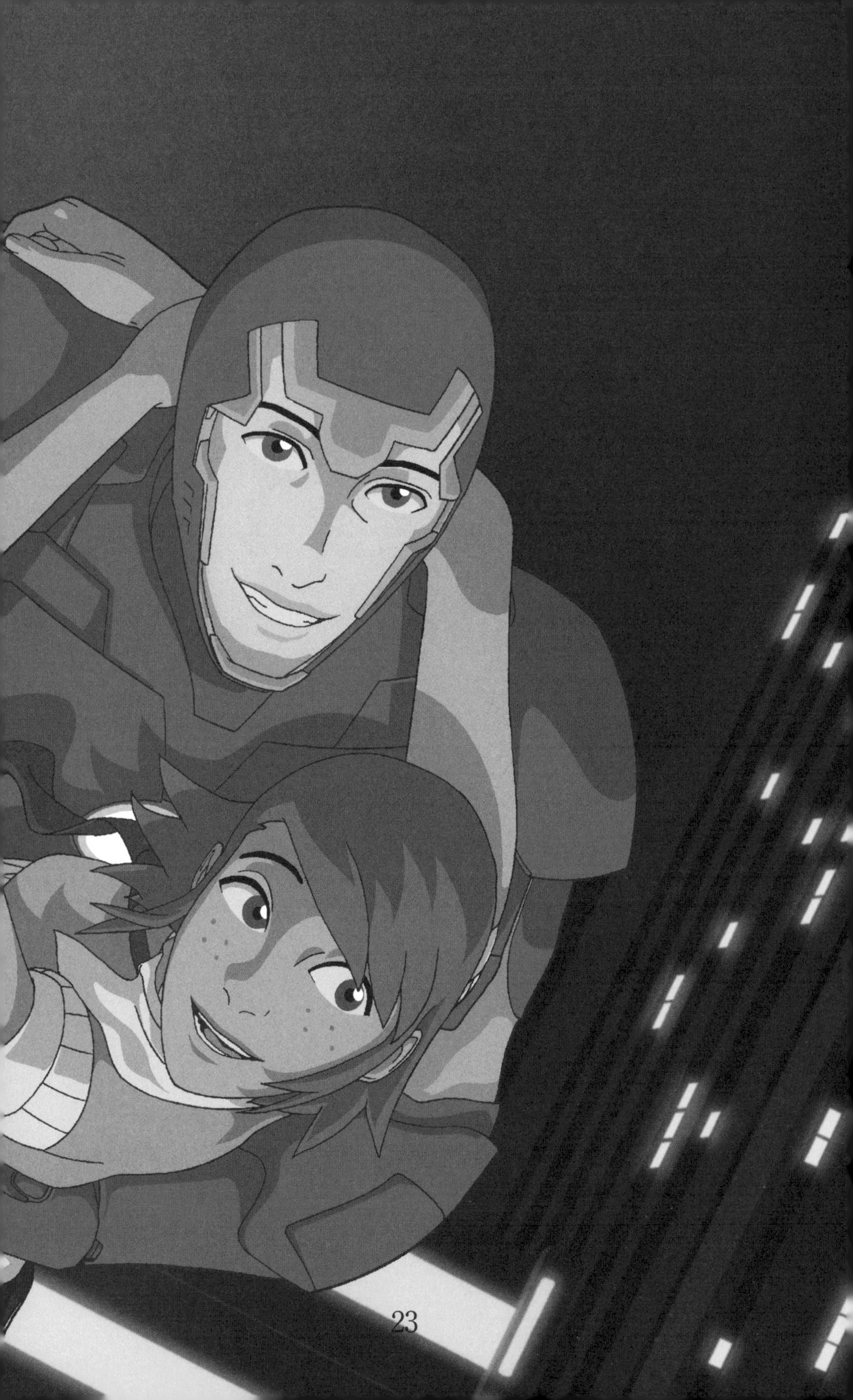

Iron Man flies

to his secret lab.

He sets Pepper down.

Whiplash is waiting

for them. He is holding

Rhodey prisoner!

Outside, Whiplash attacks Iron Man.

"Mr. Fix created *me*

to fight *you*,"

he says.

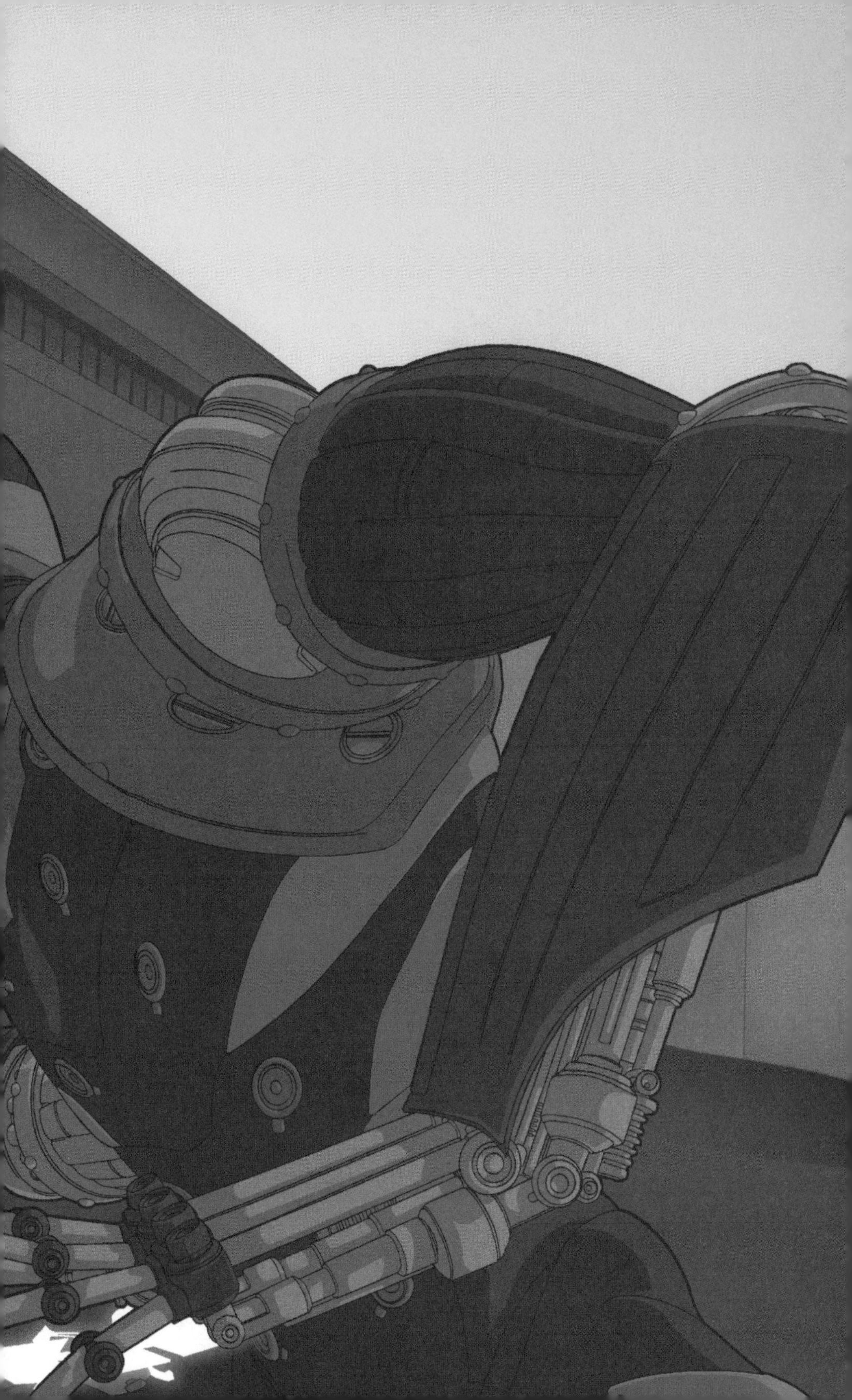

Whiplash zaps

Iron Man

with electricity.

Iron Man crashes

to the ground!

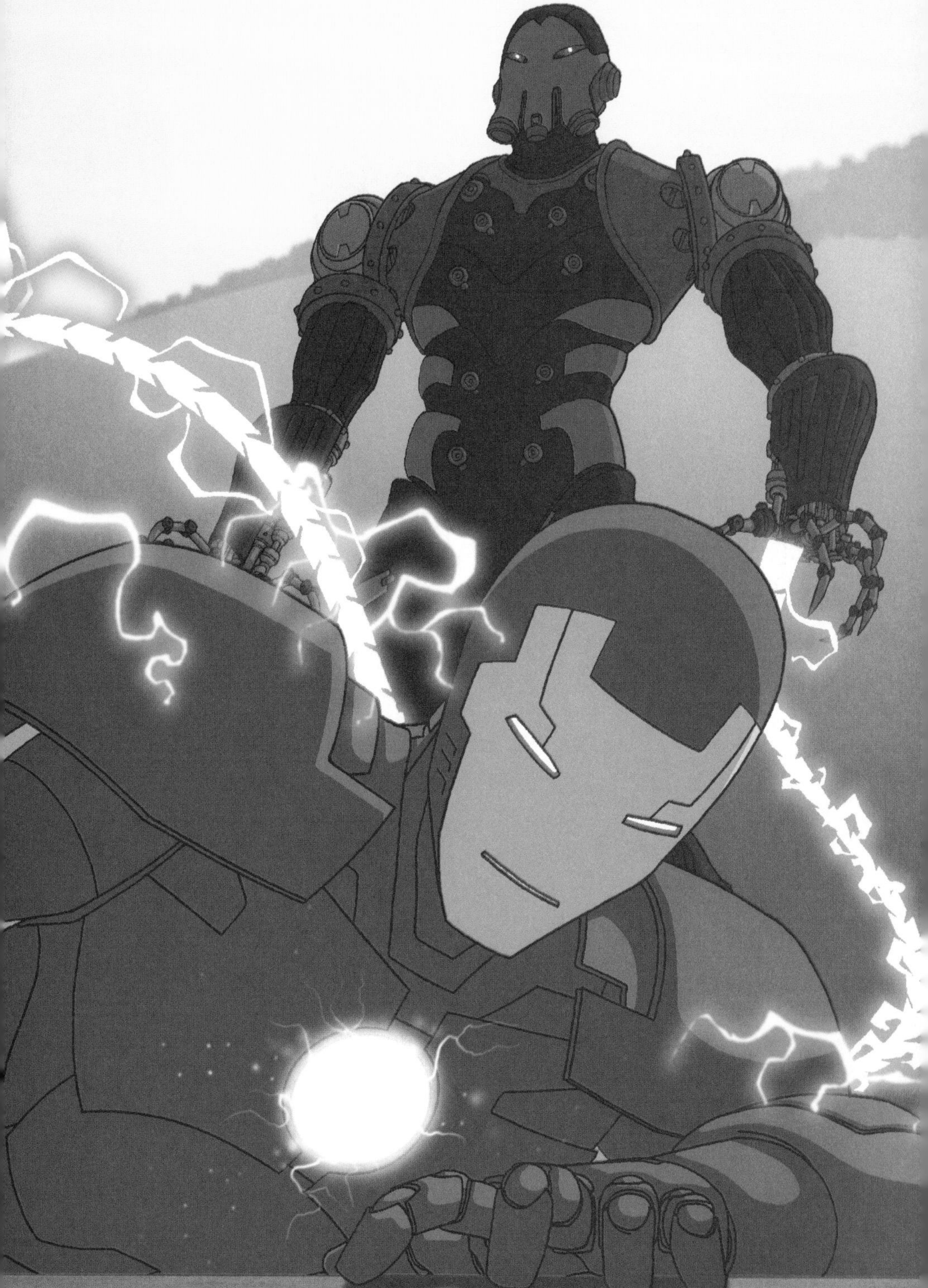

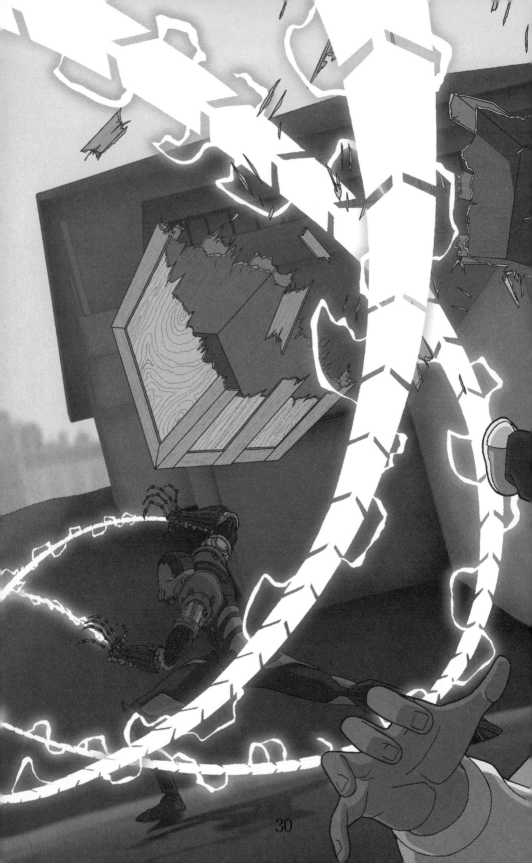

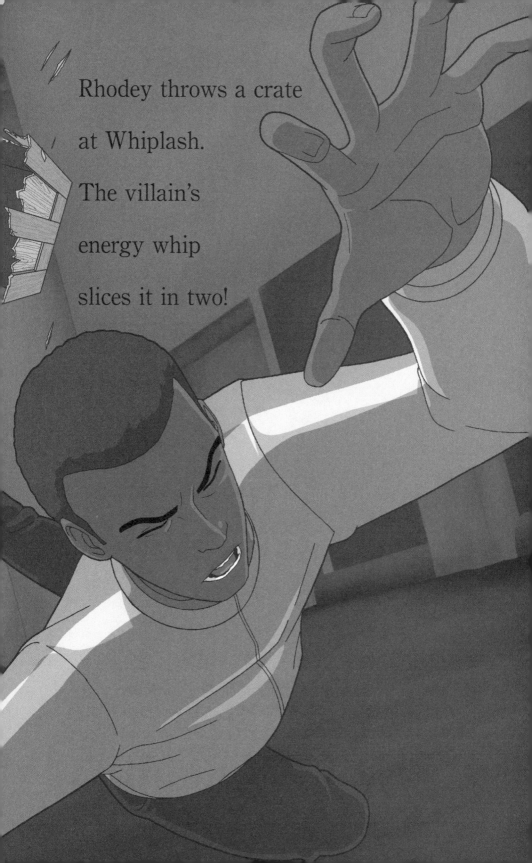

Rhodey throws a crate
at Whiplash.
The villain's
energy whip
slices it in two!

Pepper tries to help Tony.

But his armor is empty!

Whiplash follows Pepper.

She is trapped!

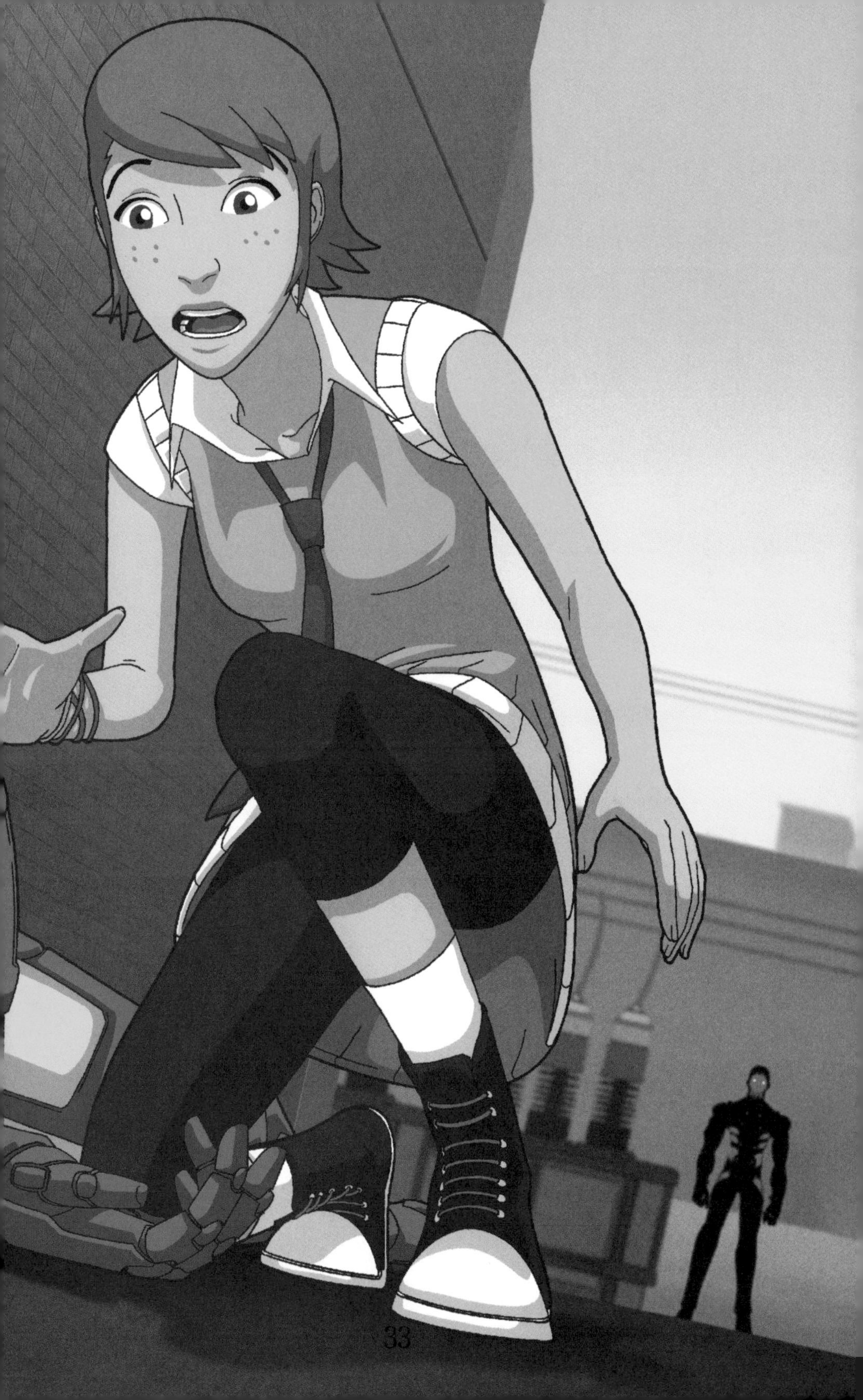

"You really should have run,"

Whiplash says.

Whiplash raises his whip!

Suddenly,

an armored fist grabs

Whiplash's energy whip!

It holds on tight!

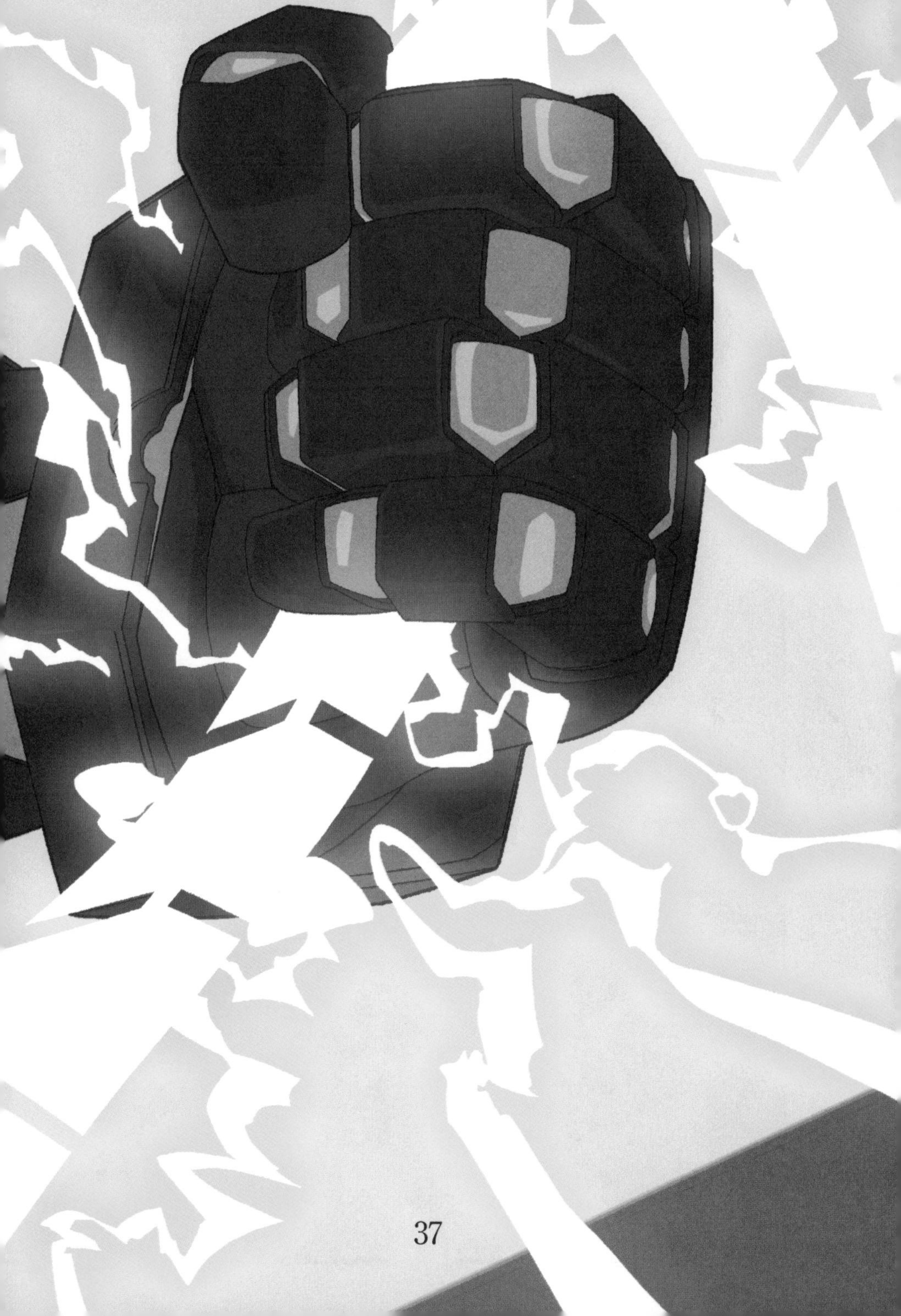

Tony is wearing

his new, more powerful

Iron Man armor!

He blasts Whiplash

with his repulsor rays.

Iron Man fires his jet boots.

He lifts Whiplash

off the ground!

Whiplash falls

onto the power lines.

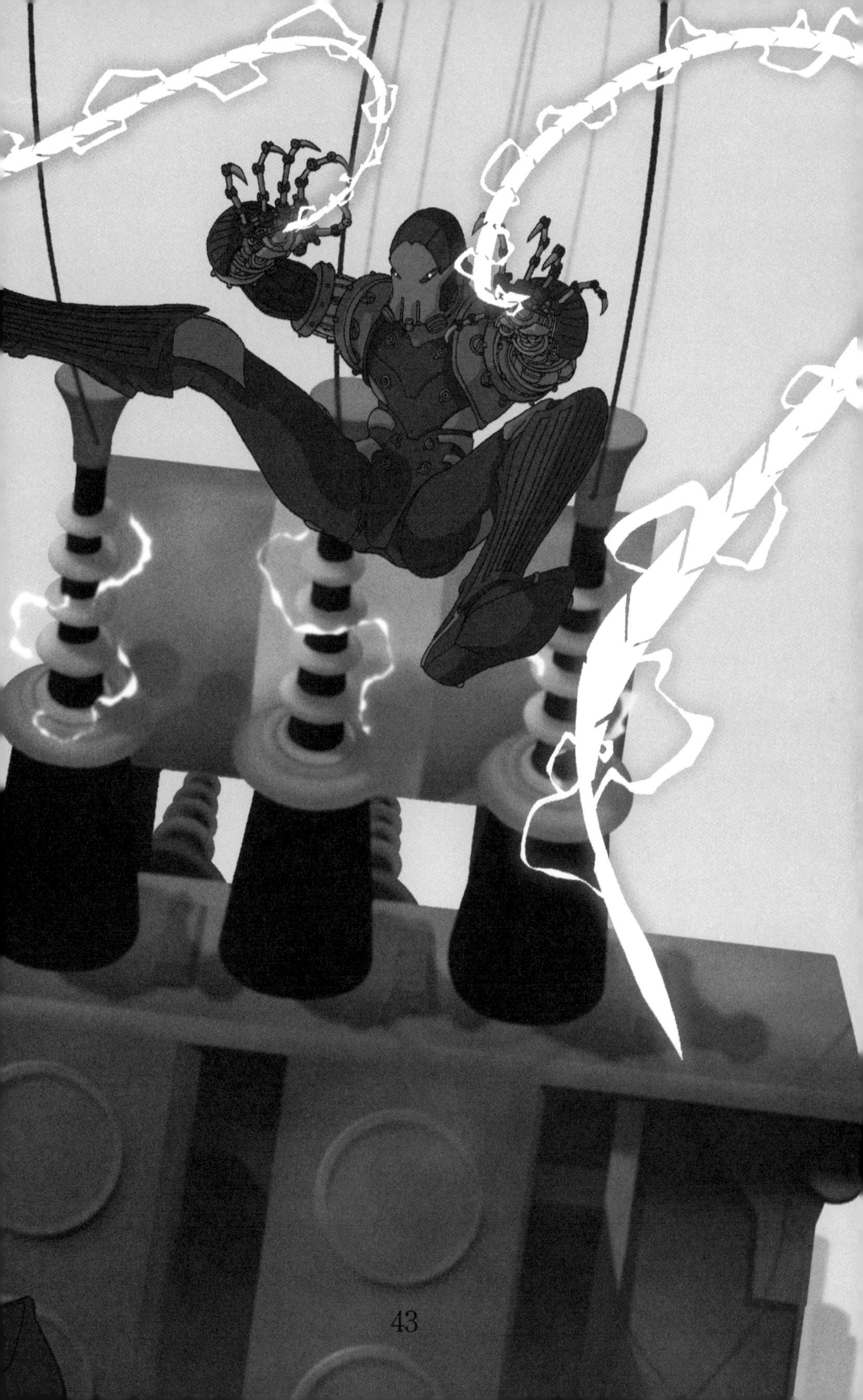

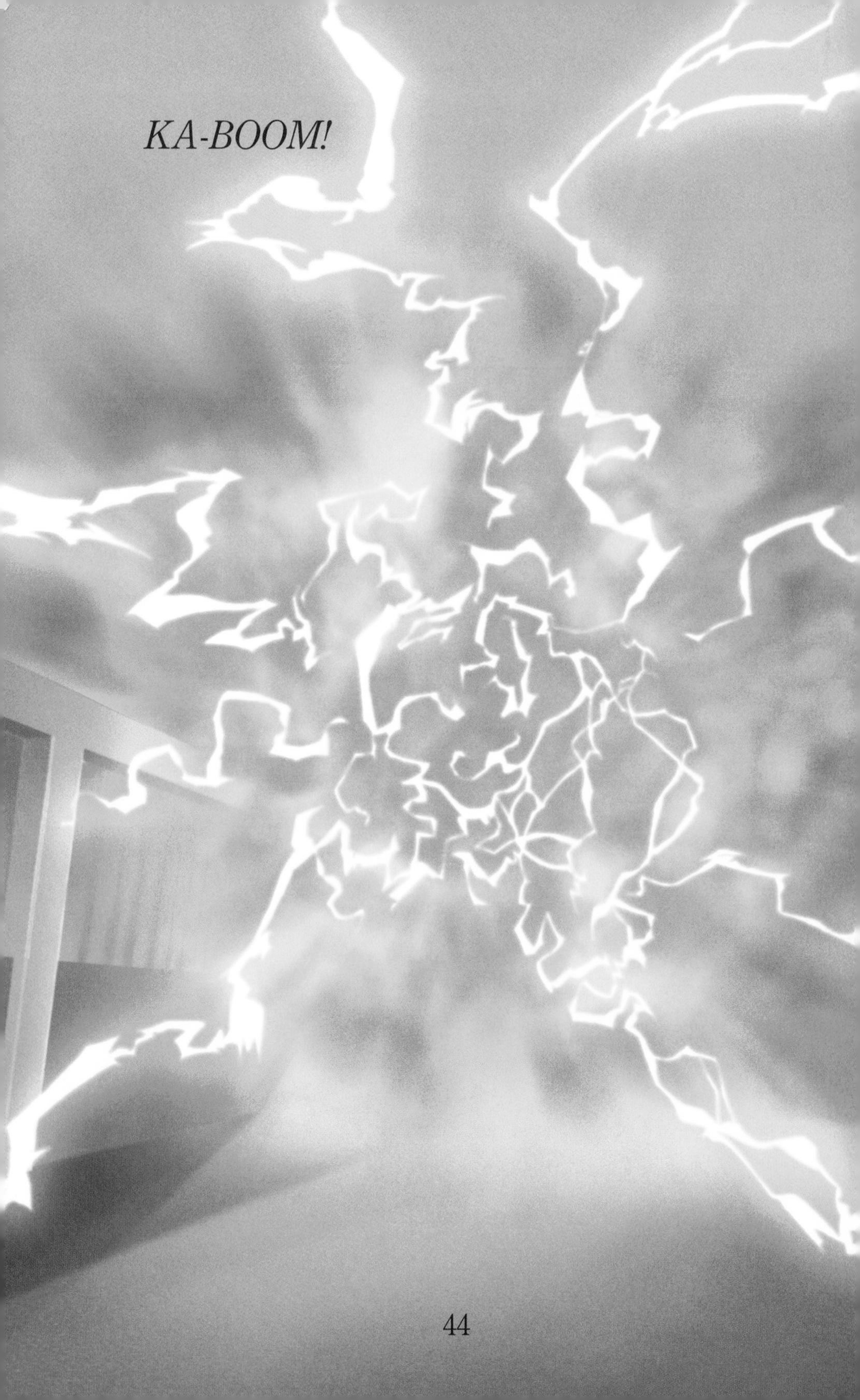
KA-BOOM!

Rhodey looks for Whiplash.

He is nowhere

to be found.

"He'll be back,"

Tony says.

"I will be ready for him—

and Mr. Fix."

"You mean *we'll* be ready,"

Pepper says.

Tony smiles.

He has the best friends ever!

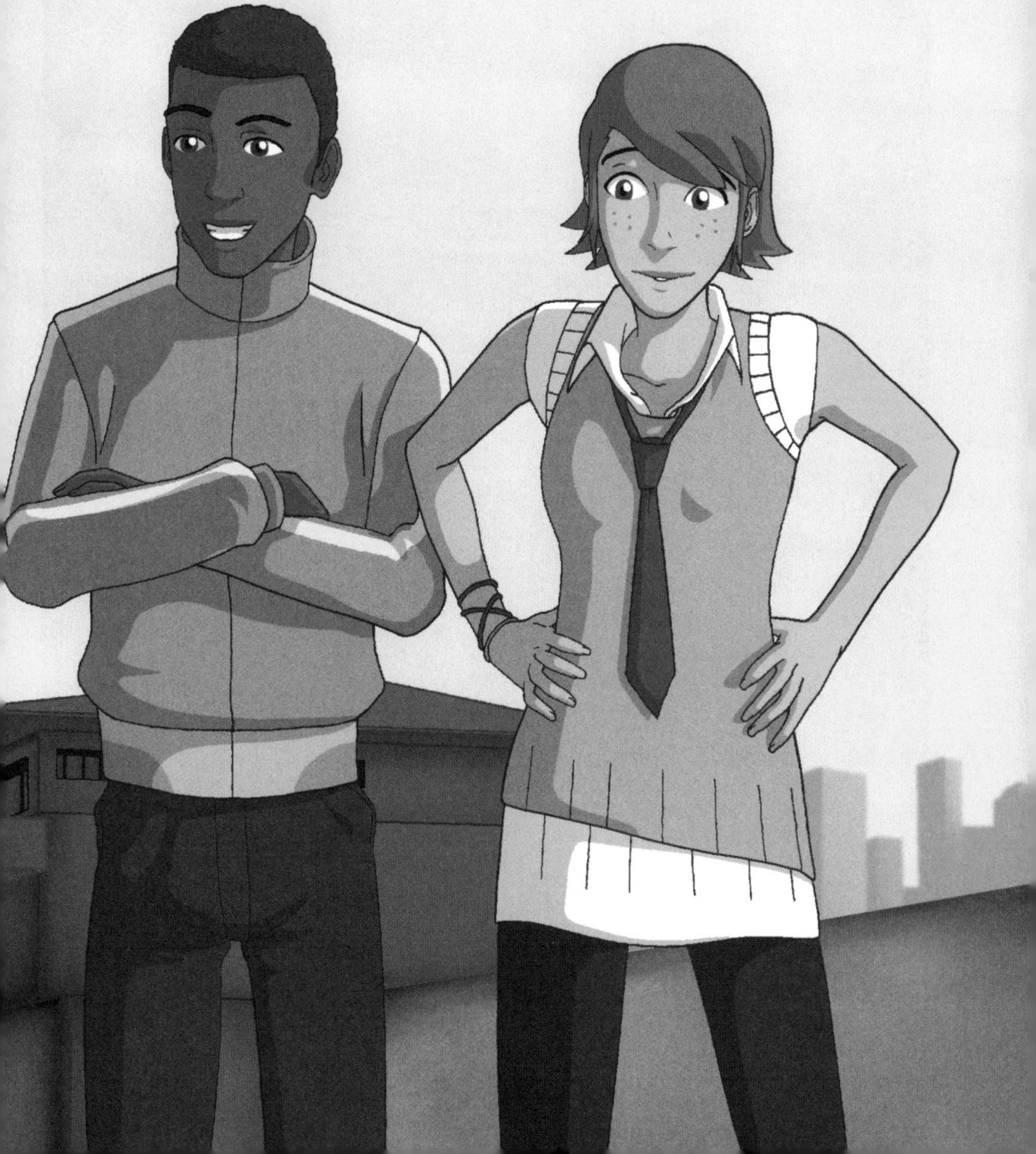

Meanwhile,

Mr. Fix prepares to fight

Iron Man another day.